Reunion

Pat Wilson

SAMUEL FRENCH

FOUNDED 1830

SAMUELFRENCH.COM
SAMUELFRENCH-LONDON.CO.UK

FOR PRODUCTION ENQUIRIES

UNITED STATES AND CANADA
Info@SamuelFrench.com
1-866-598-8449

UNITED KINGDOM AND EUROPE
Plays@SamuelFrench-London.co.uk
020-7255-4302

Each title is subject to availability from Samuel French, depending upon country of performance. Please be aware that *REUNION* may not be licensed by Samuel French in your territory. Professional and amateur producers should contact the nearest Samuel French office or licensing partner to verify availability.

Please refer to page 26 for further copyright information.

to O.G.W.

CHARACTERS

Mrs. Martha Murgatroyd	Sister of the Departed Jacob Starkie.
Miss Sarah Starkie	Sister of the Departed Jacob Starkie.
Mrs. Ellis	Who caters privately for funerals.
Mrs. Booth	An old lady who just enjoys funerals.

TIME

October 31st (Hallowe'en), one week later than Funeral Tea.

SCENE

The sitting room of a council house in a west Riding Council Estate. (Door direct to street is back stage left.)

REUNION

(When the curtain rises, the stage is rather dark. It is evening. Enter MRS. MURGATROYD SR. She lights the candles and then sits down, giving a big sigh. Enter MISS STARKIE.)

MISS STARKIE. Nay, Martha, what's that? What's illuminations for?

MRS. MURGATROYD. Why, we've got to make summat of it. We've got to make some sort of a show. We can't just leave 'im on t'sideboard, wi' t'Rent Book and t'Football Pools and them vases we won at Blackpool. Besides, it's not nice 'avin' 'm on t'sideboard.

MISS STARKIE. It's not nice 'avin' 'm on t'table! I don't know as I'm going to fancy 'avin' my dinner off it when we get shot of 'im. Ee, I do wish 'e'd been buried like a proper Christian instead of all that 'creemation' mularky.

MRS. MURGATROYD. Aye . . . it were bad enough last time. *(Gives a big sigh.)* But 'avin' to do it twice . . .

MISS STARKIE. Nay, Martha, we don't 'ave 'im creemated twice, just scattered. But I don't know that I 'olds wi' t'candles. Flowers is all right.

MRS. MURGATROYD. Aye . . . Well, we'll make sure we get t'right casket this time.

MISS STARKIE. Whear's t'other?

MRS. MURGATROYD. Outside in t'coal oil, and r'right one is on t'table, wi'candles round it.

MISS STARKIE. Why? Dust thu think it will take off, or summat? Or are we going to sing "Lead Kindly Light?"

MRS. MURGATROYD. Now, Sarah, don't get excited. Keep

thi head. If thu hadn't lost it last time we would've taken t'right casket. (*Ponders*) Ee . . . you know I thought it were funny 'im comin' out on t'cricket field nowt but black dust.

MISS STARKIE. Aye, especially wi' three green Shield stamps an' a plastic tea spoon.

MRS. MURGATROYD. Well you ought to 'ave recognized t'tea caddy, we've 'ad it long enough, it belonged to Grandma Starkie. By gum! I remember Grandfather Starkie's funeral. Buried in 'am, 'e was, and sherry and funeral biscuits. By gum! We 'ad a right do! An' there was t'reading of t'Will. Jacob were right mad when e' got nowt, 'e allus fancied t'tea caddy. Wanted it to keep 'is wine recipies in. 'Enivver gave in about it.

MISS STARKIE. Well 'e got it, an' got into it in t'end, didn't 'e?

MRS. MURGATROYD. (*Crossly.*) No 'e didn't! 'E is on t'table in 'is own tea caddy. Funny it should look just t'other one.

MISS STARKIE. Maybe t'other one were a creemation caddy in t'first place. It would have been just like Grandmother Starkie to 'ave kept it. "Waste not, want not." That were 'er motto. Maybe Great Grandfather's ashes were in it.

MRS. MURGATROYD. I wouldn't be surprised.

MISS STARKIE. Onnyhow, what are you supposed to do wi' a casket after you've scattered? Tak' it back for a refill?

MRS. MURGATROYD. (*Sharply.*) Now, Sarah, don't start that. We'd enough last time. Onnyhow, they did not creemate people in them days. It's a new-fangled idea, like long hair and t'electic ovens.

MISS STARKIE. What 'ave 'lectric ovens to do wi' it?

MRS. MURGATROYD. Well they couldn't 'ave . . . done I'm . . . not wi' t'ould side ovens . . . it took ours all day to cook a rice puddin'.

MISS STARKIE. Well people creemated each other in prehistorical times. I know, I learnt that at school.

MRS. MURGATROYD. Well Great Grandfather were old, but not that old. How old is pre-historical?

MISS STARKIE. Oh, before 'is time, I should imagine.

MRS. MURGATROYD. Aye, it would be. (*Pause.*) Ee, I wish they would come. What time is it?

MISS STARKIE. Seven o'clock.

MRS. MURGATROYD. Any way, we said seven. We'd better do it in t'dark. We don't want t'neighbours to know we 'ave to do it again. They're a right nosey lot. (*Knocking on door.*) There's someone at t'door now, it'll be Mrs. Ellis or t'other one. Go an' see who it is, Sarah. If it's t'Insurance man, tell 'im to call next week, an' if it's onnybody else tell 'em we're out. (*Miss Starkie goes to door which opens directly onto the street. Mrs. Ellis stands there.*)

MISS STARKIE. Come in, Mrs. Ellis.

MRS. MURGATROYD. An' sit you down. (*Mrs. Ellis looks apprehensively at casket.*)

MRS. ELLIS. Is that . . ?

MRS. MURGATROYD. Aye, it's Jacob.

MRS. ELLIS. Ee, fancy that. I wondered what 'ad 'appened to 'im when you went off in t'taxi wi' t' tea caddy. I couldn't catch you, so I put 'im on to t'sideboard, wi' my black scarf over 'im. Looked right nice, it did.

MRS. MURGATROYD. Yes, it were a very kind thought. (*The three ladies sit and think for a moment.*)

MRS. ELLIS. Well, Martha, what dust thu want me for? Dust thu want me to do another tea?

MRS. MURGATROYD. Nay . . . I couldn't go through all that

again.

MRS. ELLIS. Well what dust thu want? I only do funerals and weddings christenings, and you two are . . .

MRS. ELLIS. Not likely to want a wedding do, or a christening one, either. Nay, we are both past *them*. An' we are not dead, yet, though it's a wonder wi' all we've been through.

MRS. ELLIS. Oh! Well what did you want?

MRS. MURGATROYD. Well, we've 'ad a letter.

MRS. ELLIS. A letter? Who from?

MRS. MURGATROYD. From Jacob.

MRS. ELLIS. From Jacob? Then he's not dead? (*Panics.*) Who did you creemate, then? Who did you scatter? Excuse me, but I'd better go 'ome. If you creemated t'wrong chap and Jacob's still alive I'm 'avin nowt to do wi' it.

MRS. MURGATROYD. Nay . . . sit down. Jacob's dead, right enough, and we scattered nowt but a pound of tea.

MRS. ELLIS. Ee, that were a wicket waste, an' tea the price it is. But 'ow did you get a letter from him if 'e were creemated?

MRS. MURGATROYD. I found it in 'is drawers.

MRS. ELLIS. In 'is chest o' drawers?

MRS. MURGATROYD. ay, in 'is woollen ones, 'is long drawers, folded up inside, look. (*Produces a large envelope from behind the casket.*) It's got a message, on t'front of t'envelope.

MRS. ELLIS. Ee, fancy that. What does it say?

MRS. MURGATROYD. It says, "To be read out to all as is present after my send-off, after t'tea."

MRS. ELLIS. Well it's nowt to do wi' me. I'm not family, I only does teas.

MRS. MURGATROYD. (*Firmly.*) It says to be read out to *all*, and I'm doing what Jacob says, otherwise he'll turn into a haunt.

MISS STARKIE. 'E 'as already! I'll be glad when we get shot of 'im. I'm sick of having me meals on t'mangle in t'kitchen. 'E allus took up more than 'is fair share o' t'table, and now 'e's got t'lot.

MRS. MURGATROYD. (*Shocked.*) Sarah!

MRS. ELLIS. Well i don't know! This beats all. Onnyhow, there were five o' us.

MRS. MURGATROYD. Aye, well Mrs. Parker can't come, she's gone.

MRS. ELLIS. (*In a hushed voice.*) To join Jacob?

MISS STARKIE. No, to join t'old folk in Blackpool, on 'er 'olidays. It's cheaper in October. Mind you, it's noan so warm, but it's nobbut a short walk to t'Bingo on t'front.

MRS. ELLIS. Oh! Aye, and there were t'other old lass, Mrs. er . . . Mrs. er . . .

MRS. MURGATROYD. Booth. We remembered her name but not her address. So we advertised.

MRS. ELLIS. Ee, fancy that. Whear?

MRS. MURGATROYD. In the local paper. We put "Will onnyone who knows t'whereabouts of Mrs. Booth who attended the creemation tea of Mr. Jacob Starkie please ask her to call on Wednesday, October 31st at 7 pm at his house whear she will learn something to her advantage."

MISS STARKIE. I don't know what you wanted to put that for. She ain't going to get owt.O

MRS. ELLIS. Oh, Sarah! Martha was right to put that in. You always put that in a notice in t'paper.

MISS STARKIE. All she is likely to get is sceared clean out of her bloomers. I know I am.

MRS. MURGATROYD. Sarah, this is neither the time nor the place to talk about bloomers.

MISS STARKIE.   Why not? You've been goin' on about Jacob's drawers. What's t'difference? I am scared . . . getting letters from the grave!

MRS. ELLIS. (*Puzzled.*) But 'e's not in a grave. 'E were burnt up.

MISS STARKIE. (*Getting worked up.*) Well 'e should 'ave burnt 'is letters wi' 'im. Letters from the dead . . . huh! Comin' back and givin' us the creeps. Why doesn't 'e stay dead like other folks do?

MRS. MURGATROYD. Well 'e allus liked to be different, did Jacob.

MISS STARKIE. I'll say 'e did! (*Knocking on front door.*) This'll be Mother Booth.

MRS. ELLIS. I'll go an' let 'er in. (*Goes and opens door.*)

MRS. BOOTH. (*Standing in doorway, clutching umbrella.*) It's nice of you to ask me round to tea again. Ee, 'alf t'street's been round to show me t'paper. By! Nivver 'ad mi name in t'paper afore. Who is dead now? (*She comes into room and sees casket -- shouts.*) Oh, my Gord! (*She dives for door but is fielded by Mrs. Ellis.*)

MRS. ELLIS. Sit down, Mrs. Booth.

MRS. BOOTH. Not me! I'm not stoppin'! Funerals, yes, creemations *No!* I've 'ad to drink coffee since the last do. I can't face tea. And coffee gives me the wind. I's off.

MRS. MURGATROYD. Don't go, Mrs. Booth. Jacob asked for you to be 'ere.

MRS. BOOTH. (*Wildly.*) 'Ow could 'e? I told you I don't even know that I knowed 'im. I just like to go to funerals. But

I've nivver heard of a body asking for onnybody.

MRS. MURGATROYD. 'E didn't. We 'ave a letter.

MRS. BOOTH. Well l I've nivver heard of a body writing a letter, either, and what's all t'candles for? If you're going to have a see-ance I'm not stoppin'. The last one I went to t'able flew up and knocked mi glasses off, and gave me a bat in the eye. T'medium said it were Alf . . . mi 'usband . . . but 'e nivver knocked me glasses off, let alone 'it me with a table. I'd 'ave 'alf killed 'im if 'e'd so much as tried. I'm goin' 'ome, afore 'e 'as a chance to 'ave another go. And if that body in t'box is going to 'elp 'im I am goin' 'ome and I am stoppin' at 'ome in bed wi' me head under t'bedclothes . . . All Hallowe'en is bad enough wi' t'kids and their turnip lanterns scarin' t'livin' daylights out o' me, wi'out 'im.

MISS STARKIE. (*Hollowly.*) She's right . . . It is Hallowe'en. Mischief Night. Jacob is at it again!

MRS. BOOTH. (*In sepulchral voice.*) All Souls' Night. (*Points to casket with umbrella.*) When the dead rise up out of their graves, wearin' their windin' sheets. And that's what 'e's going to do.

MRS. ELLIS. 'E can't. 'E wasn't even wearin' a night shirt.

MISS STARKIE. An' if 'e was, there'd be nowt left of it.

MRS. MURGATROYD. Sit down, Mrs. Booth, and let me read you what 'e says. (*Mrs. Booth sits reluctantly, but clutches her umbrella like a sheet anchor.*) 'E writes, "To be read to all as is present after my send-off, after t'tea," and you was present, Mrs. Booth.

MRS. BOOTH. I were, by gum! And I've regretted it ivver since.

MRS. MURGATROYD. Aye well, we mun do an 'e says. (*They sit for a while in silence.*)

MRS. BOOTH. (*Truculently.*) Well? What 'appens next?

MRS. MURGATROYD.   Well, I suppose I'd better open t'envelope.

MISS STARKIE. Well you'll see nowt and know nowt if you don't. (*Mrs. Murgatroyd opens the large envelope and finds another smaller one inside.*)

MRS. MURGATROYD. Why! There's another envelope inside it, wi' writing on it.

MISS STARKIE. Well? Go on . . . what does it say?

MRS. MURGATROYD. It says, "I, Jacob Starkie demand that all the company here shall drink my health in my home-brewed wine."

MISS STARKIE. (*Snorting.*) 'Ow the 'eck can we drink 'is 'ealth when 'e's dead?

MRS. MURGATROYD. You would nivver drink 'is wine when 'e was alive.

MISS STARKIE. Neither would you. It were always boilin' and bubblin' and blowin' up and smellin' the house out.

MISS STARKIE. We can't. I poured it down t'sink.

MRS. BOOTH. Then we're sunk. 'E'll come back and haunt us!

MRS. MURGATROYD. No, I think there are two bottles in t'sideboard.   'E 'ad four, but don't you remember, two exploded!

MISS STARKIE. Aye, I do. T'bookcase fell off t'wall, and t'dog next door had a fit.

MRS. BOOTH. What did 'e put in 'em? Gunpowder?

MRS. MURGATROYD. No . . . dandelions, nettles, groundsel and cowslips, and owt else 'e could find in t'hedge.

MRS. BOOTH. I get all them for my rabbit. I hope it doesn't explode, or else bang goes mi Christmas dinner! (*Miss Starkie*

*goes to sideboard cupboard and after some rummaging returns
with two bottles.)*

MRS. BOOTH. Let's 'ave a look. (*Opens one and takes a
sip.*) Phew! Are you sure this isn't senna tea?

MRS. MURGATROYD. No, it's nettle wine.

MRS. BOOTH. (*Trying some more.*) Oh well, maybe it'll
have t'same effect . . . shouldn't wonder. What's in t'other
bottle?

MISS STARKIE. Dandelion.

MRS. BOOTH. Oh aye. Well all I can say is that too many
dandelions 'ave a very funny effect on my rabbit.

MRS. ELLIS. Such as?

MISS STARKIE. Nay, you know what we called 'em when we
were kids!

MRS. BOOTH. Oh well, let's get it over with, an' then I'll go
'ome. (Mrs. Ellis collects four glasses and pours out for all.)
I'll 'ave t'Dandelion. (*Takes glass.*) If I'd thought that this
were all I were goin' to get to my advantage I would not have
come traipsin' in the dark.

MRS. ELLIS. (*Raising her glass.*) Good health to Jacob
Starkie.

MISS STARKIE. Wherever 'e is, up or down. (*Waves her
glass up and down.*)

MRS. MURGATROYD. Mind the carpet, Sarah! When them
two bottles blew up t'drink made holes right through t'sideboard
to t'floor!

MRS. BOOTH. To Jacob. (*Drinks up, nearly chokes. They
thump her back and she mops her eyes.*) By gum! That 'as a
kick. It nearly killed me! Are yo sure it isn't brass polish?

MISS STARKIE. (*Trying hers.*) No, it tastes more like paint
remover. I rather like it. I'll have another.

MRS. BOOTH. (*Admiringly.*) By gosh, lass! You've got a stronger stomach than I've got. (*The others sip theirs. Miss Starkie sits down with bottle and keeps refilling her glass.*) Well, is that all?

MRS. MURGATROYD. No. I'll open t'other envelope.

MRS. ELLIS. Aye, do. (*Mrs. Murgatroyd opens envelope.*)

MRS. MURGATROYD. Why, it's a Will!

MISS STARKIE. (*With an explosive hiccup.*) A Will? What 'ad Jacob to leave? T'house is rented and we spent t'insurance money on t'cree . . . on the cree . . . on the cree . . . on t'other do.

MRS. BOOTH. Well, what does 'e say?

MRS. MURGATROYD. It says, "I, Jacob Elkanah Starkie, being of sound mind . . ."

MISS STARKIE. There's a laugh! 'E were proper daft! Daft as a brush.

MRS. MURGATROYD. That's enough, Sarah. nivver speak ill o' t'dead or they'll come back an' haunt you.

MISS STARKIE. (*Standing up and leaning her elbow on casket.*) Shtrikes me 'e hash, and if e'sh going to shpend t'resh of hish life, or my life, plonk in t'middle o' t'table I'm going to use 'im as a shentre piece.

MRS. ELLIS. For shame, Sarah! Go on, Martha.

MRS. MURGATROYD. ". . . being of sound mind do bequeath all my money to my sisters and to any friends who turn up at my send-off I leave ten pounds apiece. But as I hereby state that I never had any friends during my lifetime I shall be interested to see who turns up when I'm dead."

MRS. ELLIS. Why did 'e put that? 'Ow can 'e be 'ere to see who's 'ere when 'e's dead?

MISS STARKIE. (*Slowly and deliberately waving her bottle.*)

But 'e ish 'ere. Plonk in t'middle o' t'table. Preshi . . . preshi . . . preshiding over this booze-up. Shilly old idiot! Or maybe not sho shilly. 'Ave a drink, Jacob. (*Pours drips of wine onto casket.*)

MRS. MURGATROYD. Sarah! Don't get hysterical, I beg you.

MISS STARKIE. Not hysterical, but if we can't get rid of 'im we might as well put 'im in a pickle.

MRS. BOOTH. Maybe this *is* a see-ance. Come to think of it, there might be summat in it. Alf might 'ave knocked my glasses off to see if it were me. I 'ad a different pair when 'e were alive. Mind you, 'e could 'ave used something different from a table to clout me wi'. I 'ad a black eye for weeks. Oh well, I'll 'ave mi ten pounds and go.

MISS STARKIE. We don't know where it is. I haven't sheen any money. Ish there any more of t'Will, Martha?

MRS. MURGATROYD. Yes. (*Reads.*) "I direct that my ashes be scattered on t'cricket pitch so that my dust will mingle with the grass until I rise up to heaven on the glorious day of resurrection."

MRS. BOOTH. 'E'll 'ave a job.

MRS. MURGATROYD. Why?

MRS. BOOTH. 'Cos they railed off t'pitch today. It's going to be high rise flats. 'E'll soon be under tons of concrete if you put 'im there. Ee, think of it. T'great Day o' Judgement and 'im trying to heave t'ten storey flats off 'is chest!

MRS. ELLIS. Well we mun take 'im to t'Cemetery and scatter 'im there.

MISS STARKIE. It's pitch black outshide, black as inshide o' t'mill chimney, an' if you think I'm going prowling round a shemetery clutching Jacob to mi bosom on All Hallowe'en, you are mistaken. (*Takes another drink.*)

MRS. MURGATROYD. Well we must put 'im somewhere.

MISS STARKIE. (*Now has difficulty focussing and can't hit glass.*) Put me another drink in my glass. It won't shtay still.

MRS. ELLIS. (*Pours the last of the bottle into the glass.*) If we all went to the Cemetery together it might be all right. I 'ave an old pram. We could put 'im in that.

MISS STARKIE. (*Shouting and waving the bottle.*) Shnorrabirragood! Shemetery ish shurt. Early closhing. Shut the shemetery when it'sh dark, keep the shpooks in and ush out. We will have to climb over the gatesh or the railingsh, and that ish imposhible. All got casht iron shpikes and shpears on t'top.

MRS. MURGATROYD. Sarah! You're drunk.

MISS STARKIE. Yesh! Good old Jacob. I know, let'sh take 'im to t'shemetery and chuck 'im over t'gate.

MRS. MURGATROYD. (*Indignantly.*) I'm not havin' my brother chucked over anything, least of all a cemetery. Chucked over, indeed!

MISS STARKIE. I don't see why not, 'e got chucked out o't'Star and Garter every Saturday night. It'sh only what 'e'sh used to.

MRS. BOOTH. Why not just put 'im on t'fire?

MISS STARKIE. (*Staggering over to Mrs. booth.*) Can't do that, already done that. Can't be creemated twice. Beshides, you'd put t'fire out. You put coal on t'fire, not ashes, and 'e's nothing but asher . . . asher . . . asher . . . what was I going to say?

MRS. BOOTH. All fall down?

MISS STARKIE. No! He's nothing but ashesh, nothing but ashesh in the box, and 'ish four teeth.

MRS. MURGATROYD. (*Horrified.*) Sarah, how do you know?

MISS STARKIE. Shimple. Jusht opened the box, and there they were, shame old teeth, one here, one there. one here, one there, shame as ever.

MRS. MURGATROYD. But Sarah, why did you open the box?

MISS STARKIE. 'Cos I wanted to be shure. Never know, we might 'ave scattered Jacob after all, both boxes exactly alike. Beshides, I forgot 'e was in it, and I wanted a cup o' tea. I mean, we've used it as t'tea caddy for donkeys years. Go on readin', Martha. What else does he shay?

MRS. MURGATROYD. (*Peering at paper.*) It's awfully difficult to read. 'Is writing is terrible. T'pen nib must 'a' got crossed. Why didn't 'e use a ball-point?

MISS STARKIE. 'E was too mean to buy owt.

MRS. BOOTH. Well maybe he was like me -- had nowt but's Pension.

MRS. MURGATROYD. (*Still trying to make out Will.*) It says "The money is in my . . ."

MRS. ELLIS. Well, go on.

MRS. MURGATROYD. I can't, there's a blot.

MRS. BOOTH. 'Ere, let me 'ave a look. (*Peers at it.*) It says, "The money is in my books..)

MRS. MURGATROYD. (*Astonished.*) Books? What books?

MRS. BOOTH. 'Ow should I know, 'e weren't my brother.

MISS STARKIE. (*Rising with difficulty and going to bookshelf.*) I shall have a look. (*She hands out books as she talks. The others open them, shake them, and throw them down.*) We have the Bible, that's for you. (*Hands out.*) The Railway timetable for 1906, Ol' Moore's Almanack, t'Clock Almanack, the Gardener's World . . . Little Women and Good Wives . . . makes me cry, shtill, poor Beth dying so young, (*Sobs, mops eyes and blows nose.*) and Pig Keeper's Weekly.

Did we ever poshesh a pig, Martha?

MRS. MURGATROYD. No, of course not. Don't be fond. Where would we put it?

MISS STARKIE. I don't know . . . poor little piggy, nowhere to shelter and nowhere to go. (*Sobs.*)

MRS. MURGATROYD. Pull yourself together, Sarah.

MISS STARKIE. Yesh. We musht keep cheerful, mushn't we? Here are two library books. Jacob should have taken them back months and months and months ago. And there is the dish . . . the dish . . . the dishionary, an' that'sh the lot. (*All search through the books, leaving them all over the floor.*)

MRS. ELLIS. Well, there's definitely nothing in this lot.

MISS STARKIE. I dishtinctly remember another book somewhere. It'sh propping up a chair in Jacob's bedroom. (*Confidentially to Mrs. Booth.*) One leg's shorter than the other . . . the chair's, I mean, not Jacob's. Or the floor is not straight, which is more than poshible, we get a lot of shub . . . . er . . . shub . . . er . . . shubshidence.

MRS. MURGATROYD. Subside yourself, Sarah. You ought to be ashamed of yourself. I'll go and get the book. Sit down before you fall down. (*Miss Sharkie capsizes into a chair and Mrs. Murgatroyd goes off right.*)

MRS. BOOTH. (*To Mrs. Ellis.*) Ee, I' opes she finds it. Ten pounds would be right champion. I'll put most of it away for Christmas, but I'll send my grandson in Australia a book.

MRS. ELLIS. Oh! Have you a grandson? You did tell us you had a son out there.

MRS. BOOTH. Oh aye, 'e 'as a little lad.

MRS. ELLIS. What's 'e like?

MRS. BOOTH. Ee, right champion, a grand little lad. Aah've nivver seen 'im. Don't suppose Ah ivver will, but 'e sent me a picture last Christmas. Painted it himself, he did. I don't rightly know which way up it is, but it's right bonny.

MRS. ELLIS. By gum! I bet you prize that.

MRS. BOOTH. Aye, I do an' all. Ah've got it up on t'mantelshelf whear ivveryone can see it. (*Re-enter Mrs. Murgatroyd with a book.*)

MRS. MURGATROYD. Here it is. It's t'Telephone Directory for London, A to D, 1956.

MISS STARKIE. Why have we got a telephone directory for London? We don't poshesh a telephone.

MRS. MURGATROYD. Because it went for a penny at t'Church jumble sale. Jacob bought it. He thought 'e might read it during long winter evenings, but 'e nivver did.

MRS. BOOTH. And now 'e nivver will.

MISS STARKIE. It were a daft thing to buy. Shtill, it came in useful for holding 'is chair up. (*Takes it and searches through.*) There's no money in it, but look! There's shix pages of Browns. Ishn't it shad?

MRS. ELLIS. What is sad? You mean because there's no money in it?

MISS STARKIE. No, all those Browns, and no one knows which is which. (*Shakes the book.*) No pounds, only browns, nothing at all anywhere. Jacob is pulling our legsh. Let'sh chuck 'im into t'shemetery and go to bed.

MRS. ELLIS. Let me have another look at t'Will.

MRS. BOOTH. You'll see nowt that I can't. i've 'ad these glasses for thirty years, and they are as good as the day I bought them at Woolworth's.

MRS. ELLIS. Well, that's as may be. (*Holds paper up to the light.*) Looks like boots to me.

MISS STARKIE. Did you shay boots?

MRS. MURGATROYD. Jacob allus stuffed 'is boots wi' paper when they were wet . . . do you think . . . ?

MISS STARKIE. You gave all Jacob's boots away yeshterday, to the Vicar for the Jumble Sale.

MRS. MURGATROYD. Oh my goodness! So I did.

MRS. ELLIS. Ee, my! When is t'Jumble Sale?

MISS STARKIE. (*Standing up and waving her arms about.*) On All Saints' Day. Church allus has a Jumble Sale on All Saints' Day, because the church is All Saints' Church. Although what the saints want with a lot of old clothes and whatnots and doodahs I can't think.

MRS. BOOTH. Aye, well it's All Saints' Day tomorrow.

MRS. ELLIS. Go and ring the Vicar up, and tell him to stop it until he's 'ad a look in Jacob's boots.

MRS. BOOTH. (*Urgently.*) Aye, do. Here is t'telephone book.

MISS STARKIE. In the first place, the Vicar does not live in London, and shecondly the nearest telephone box is half a mile away, and lastly I don't know the Vicar's name.

MRS. ELLIS. (*Crossly.*) You *must* know the Vicar's name. What do you call 'im when he comes to see you?

MISS STARKIE. Vicar. We just call 'im Vicar. 'E answers very well to that.

MRS. BOOTH. Well look in the Parish magazine. His name's sure to be on t'front o' that.

MISS STARKIE. Do, by all means, do. (*She staggers over to sideboard, pulls a drawer out and empties contents on to the floor, sees something and gets down on her hands and knees.*) Ah, there it is.

MRS. BOOTH. Well, what's 'is name?

MISS STARKIE. I can not tell you. I was referring to the fact that there'sh my knitting pattern. I losht it when I was doing the front of my jumper. And the front's not like the back at all.

MRS. MURGATROYD. Oh, for goodness sake! You've been knitting yon' jumper for years. Where the heck is t'magazine? (*They all rummage madly.*) Here it is.

MRS. ELLIS. Well, what's 'is name?

MRS. MURGATROYD. Smith. Go and ring 'im up, Sarah.

MISS STARKIE. Thish ish going to take all night, finding out which Smish, Smish wish, Oh Smith! I might point out that it'sh raining cats and dogs.

MRS. MURGATROYD. Well, put your boots on.

MISS STARKIE. They're at t'cobblers.

MRS. MURGATROYD. Well put mine on.

MISS STARKIE. Can't. they're two shizes too shmall.

MRS. MURGATROYD. Well put Jacob's on.

MRS. BOOTH. I thought you'd given them away?

MISS STARKIE. Not 'is wellies. A scarecrow wouldn't thank you for them. They're in t'coal 'oil, I imagine, where they allus were.

MRS. MURGATROYD. I'll go and get them. You get your mac. (*Exits through front door.*)

MISS STARKIE. Why do I always get the daft jobs? Shmith. T'town's full o' Shmiths. (*Exits SR muttering.*)

MRS. BOOTH. Ee, I do 'ope she gets there afore t'Vicar gives them boots away.

MRS. ELLIS. So do I. By, what I could do wi' ten pounds!

MRS. BOOTH. Aye, well, if Jacob meant us to have it we'll 'ave it.

MRS. ELLIS. Pity we didn't 'ave a see-ance.

MRS. BOOTH. Aye, let's try.

MRS. ELLIS. Ee, dare we?

MRS. BOOTH. (*Tapping casket with umbrella.*) Are you there, Jacob Starkie? If thu wants us to 'ave ten pounds, knock twice. (*There is a double knock on front door, as Miss Starkie re-enters wearing mac. She goes to open front door. In a panic.*) Don't answer t'door. Jacob's out there!

MISS STARKIE. Don't be shilly, it'll be Martha wi' 'is boots. (*She opens door and Mrs. Murgatroyd enters with a boot in each hand.*)

MRS. MURGATROYD. 'Ere you are, Sarah. A walk will clear your 'ead.

MISS STARKIE. (*Sitting and trying to put a boot on.*) Either my feet 'ave grown or these boots 'ave shrunk. I can't get them on.

MRS. MURGATROYD. Don't be helpless and hopeless, Sarah.

MISS STARKIE. (*Struggling.*) Shnot a bit o'good. There's something in them. they feel as if they're full of Jacob's feet.

MRS. MURGATROYD. (*Taking one and plunging a hand into it and pulling out paper money.*) They're stuffed wi' paper . . . *Money!* Look -- notes!

MRS. BOOTH. Well by gum! So Jacob weren't such a bad old stick after all.

MRS. MURGATROYD. No, look . . . pound notes! Five-pound notes!!!

MISS STARKIE. Well take them out, and then I can get the bootsh on and ring Vicar Shmith, if I can find his blashted number.

MRS. MURGATROYD. We don't need to. We've found the money!

MISS STARKIE. Hipsh hipsh hurray! How much?

MRS. MURGATROYD. Poundsh and poundsh . . . dang it,

Sarah, you've got me doing it!

MISS STARKIE. Sherves you right for getting drunk.

MRS. MURGATROYD. Oh really! Here, Mrs. Booth, here is your money, and you too, Mrs. Ellis.

MRS. ELLIS. Thank you very much, I'm sure.

MRS. BOOTH. Ee, I can't get over it! By, 'e mun 'a been a good man. I's not frightened o' 'im onny more. I tell you what, I'll take t'ashes an' scatter 'em as i go 'ome. I'll scatter 'em on nettles and dandelions, then maybe we'll drink 'im in some 'ome-made winde someday, same as we did in t'tea afore.

MRS. MURGATROYD. That's right kindly of you.

MRS. BOOTH. Nay it's nowt. It's first time in my life anyone 'as given me owt for nowt. Give us a paper bag and we'll put Jacob in it.

MRS. ELLIS. Is there any more writin' in t'Will?

MRS. MURGATROYD. Ee, we forgot to finish readin' it! Yes, it says, ". . . and having provided for my sisters, who provided reluctantly for me, I shall now depart in peace and maybe trouble them no more."

MISS STARKIE. What's 'e mean, "trouble us no more?" 'E was nowt much trouble. T'trouble is, I miss fratchin' wi' 'im. What's 'e mean by "maybe?"

MRS. ELLIS. (*Who has been rummaging on the floor.*) Well here's a paper bag. We'll all stand round reverently. (*They do.*)

MISS STARKIE. I'm going to sing a hymn.

MRS. BOOTH. Aye, do, and we'll all join in.

MISS STARKIE. (*Singing at the top of her voice.*)
WE PLOUGH THE FIELDS AND SCATTER
OUR JACOB ON THE GROUND,

FOR WE NEVER KNOW WHERE
HE WILL NEXT BE FOUND.
WE FIND HIM IN THE COFFEE,
WE FIND HIM IN THE TEA,
BUT IF HE STOPS ON T'TABLE
HE'LL BE TOO MUCH FOR ME!
    MRS. MURGATROYD. Ee, our Sarah! May you be forgiven!

    MISS STARKIE. (*She takes the bag.*) Oh well, depart in peace, Jacob. (*The others stand with bowed heads as she opens the box and then slams the lid down with a crash. She can't believe her eyes.*)

    MRS. BOOTH. Well go on, what's the matter?

    MISS STARKIE. (*Hollowly.*) He has!

    MRS. MURGATROYD. He has what?

    MISS STARKIE. Gone! Departed in peace. There's nowt in t'box. Bone wi' the wind.

    MRS. BOOTH. No wonder, if he drank 'is 'ome-made wine. But whear is he?

    MISS STARKIE. 'E's done it again! He'll be in t'box in t'coal 'oil. (*Stage darkens. There is a ghostly laugh. Black out.*)

* * *

GLOSSARY

All Hallowe'en -- All Souls' Night
Clout -- hit
Coal 'oil -- coal shed (coal hole)
Fond -- daft or stupid
Fratchin' -- fighting
Groundsel -- a common British weed
Ivver -- ever
Mularky -- a daft performance
Nivver -- never
Nowt -- nothing
Owt -- anything, something
Senna tea -- a laxative made from leaves of senna and infused
    in hot water
Side oven -- Baking oven to one side of a coal cooking range.
Traipsin' -- wandering about
Wellies -- Wellington boots, gumboots
Wind -- flatulence
Woollen drawers -- long underpants (long johns)

MUSIC USE NOTE

Licensees are solely responsible for obtaining formal written permission from copyright owners to use copyrighted music in the performance of this play and are strongly cautioned to do so. If no such permission is obtained by the licensee, then the licensee must use only original music that the licensee owns and controls. Licensees are solely responsible and liable for all music clearances and shall indemnify the copyright owners of the play(s) and their licensing agent, Samuel French, against any costs, expenses, losses and liabilities arising from the use of music by licensees. Please contact the appropriate music licensing authority in your territory for the rights to any incidental music.

IMPORTANT BILLING AND CREDIT REQUIREMENTS

If you have obtained performance rights to this title, please refer to your licensing agreement for important billing and credit requirements.